First Time

At

The Pool

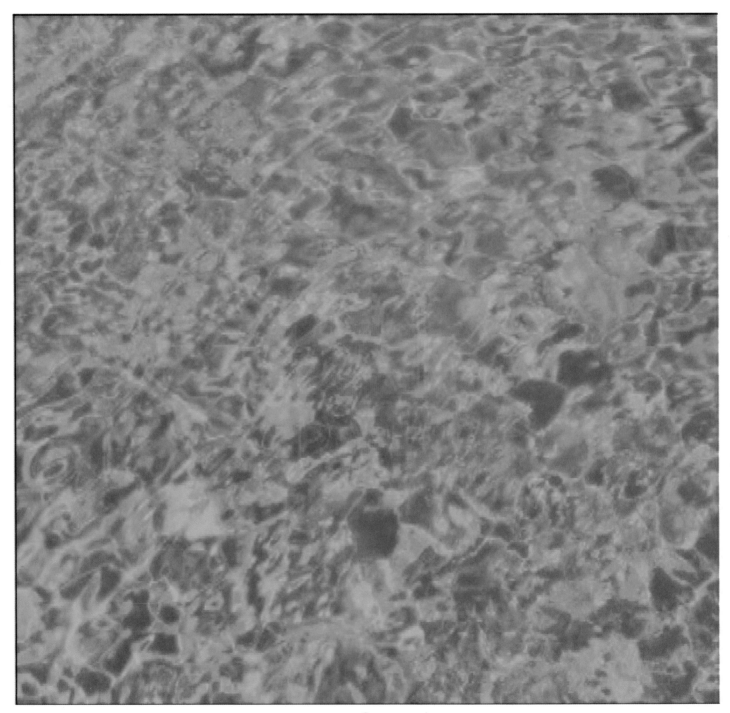

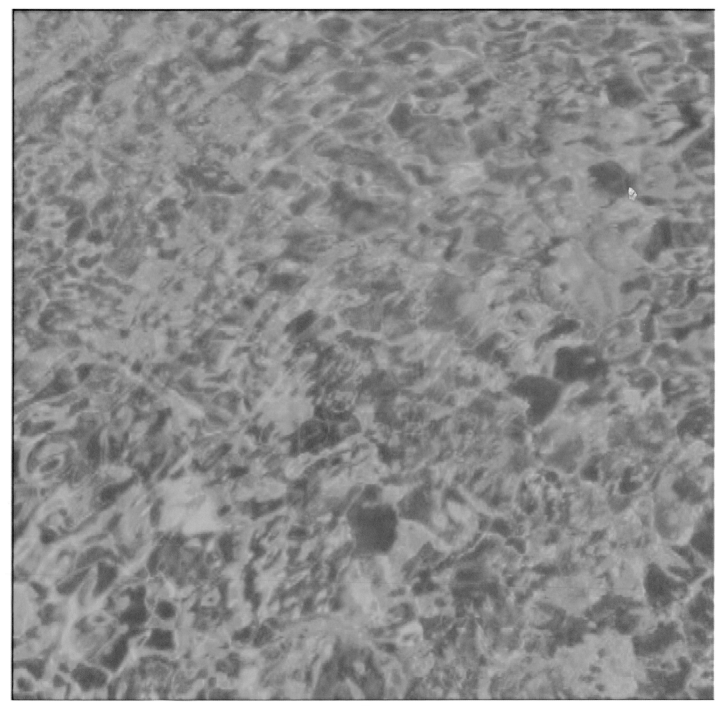

3

First Time At The Pool

Written by: RyAnn Adams Hall

Illustrated by: Inga Shalvashvili

First published in the US 2014 by CreateSpace, a DBA of On-Demand Publishing, LLC.

ISBN-13: 978-1500383589
ISBN-10: 1500383589

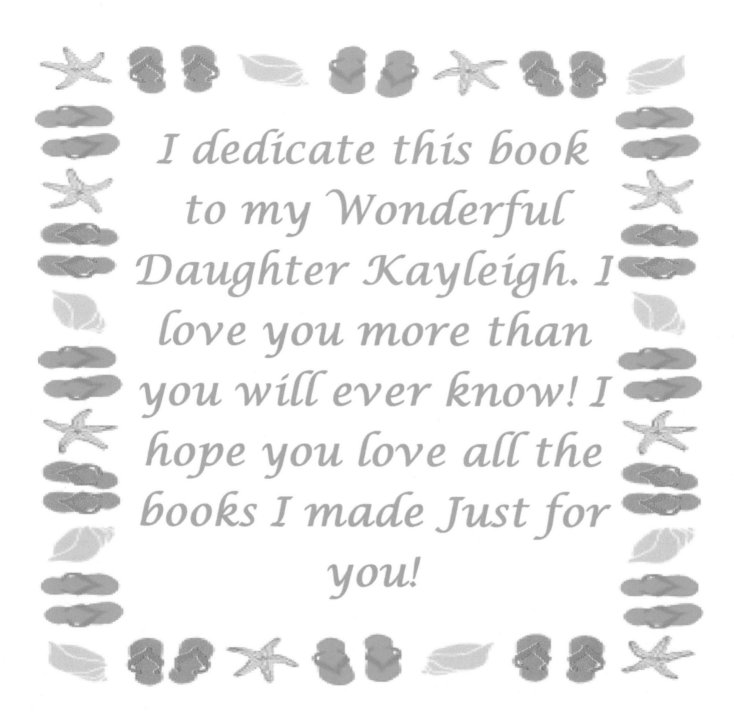

I dedicate this book to my Wonderful Daughter Kayleigh. I love you more than you will ever know! I hope you love all the books I made Just for you!

This Book Belongs To:

~~~~~~~~~~~~~~~~~~~~~~~~~~~~~~~~~~

Kayleigh is only two years old. She loves to play in water more than anything in the world. She loves her baby pool so much that Mommy decides she may be ready for the big pool.

So one day, Mommy and Daddy take her to the big pool. She is not scared at all. As soon as she sees the pool, she gets so excited and starts screaming, "Water! Water!" Mommy has to hold Kayleigh tight to keep her from running strait into the pool.

Mommy has to put Kayleigh's pink floaties on her before she can get into the pool. Kayleigh does not know that she cannot stand up and touch the bottom of the big pool without her head going under water.

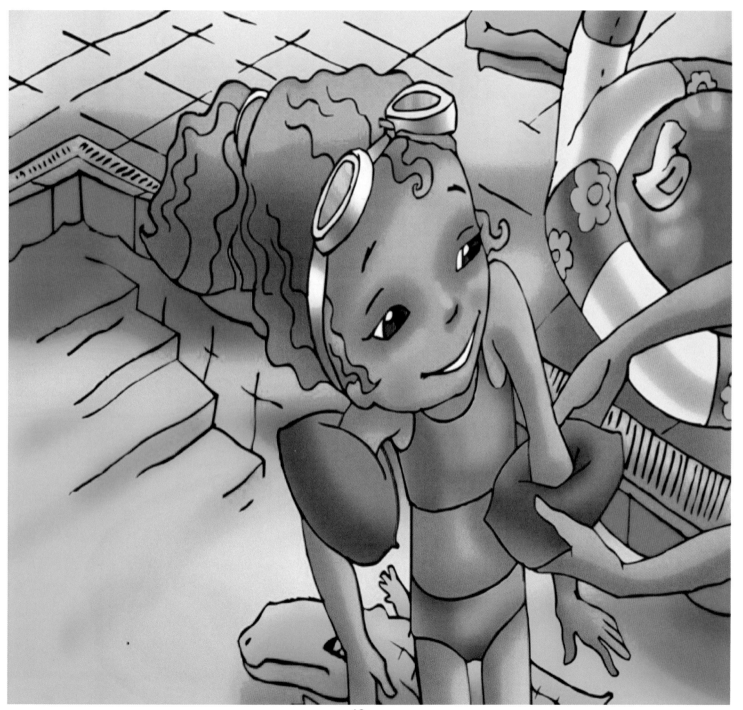

As soon as mommy gets Kayleigh's floaties on her, she takes off running for the pool! She walks down the stairs and gets in the pool without hesitation. She is so excited for her first time in the big pool that she is not scared at all.

Mommy swims with Kayleigh and stays nearby her just in case she needs help. She swims around the pool on her own and does not need Mommy or Daddy's help at all! She has so much fun playing with all the pool toys.

She kicks her little feet and uses her arms, one after the other, to pull herself around the pool. She is a natural born swimmer. As Kayleigh is swimming around the pool, she watches as the big girls are diving off the edge of the pool into the water.

She laughs and thinks that looks like so much fun! She decides to walk up the stairs and gets out of the pool. Mommy watches Kayleigh as she stands at the edge of the pool looking down at the water. She wants to jump in too like the big girls.

Kayleigh is brave! She starts smiling and jumps right off the edge into the pool! Kayleigh goes under the water and floats back up to the top of the water. Mommy grabs her and looks at her to make sure she is ok.

Well what do you know! She sure is. She has the biggest smile on her face. It did not scare her at all to go under the water or get water in her face. She wants to get out of the pool and do it again. Mommy and Daddy are so proud of Kayleigh.

She swims around that pool like a pro. When it is time to go home, Kayleigh is very sad. She does not want to get out of the pool. She had so much fun swimming in the big pool. Mommy tells her that they will come back to swim again one day soon.

Other Children's Books by Mrs. Hall!

A Swing Set for her Birthday

Caden Loves His Momma

Rylie's New Bike

Shelby Loves Candy

Abbie Goes to the Zoo

Three Little Sisters

Seasons Come, Seasons Go

Valentine's Crushed

Night Night My Child

Not Another Rainy Day

Butterfly's Big Adventure

A Puppy For Christmas

http://ryannhall3691.wix.com/childrens-books#

http://www.facebook.com/ryannadamshall

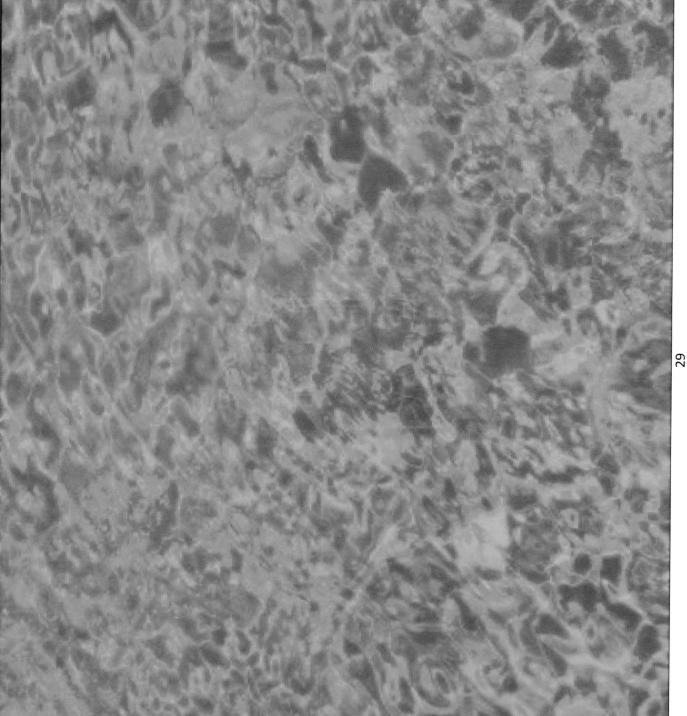

29

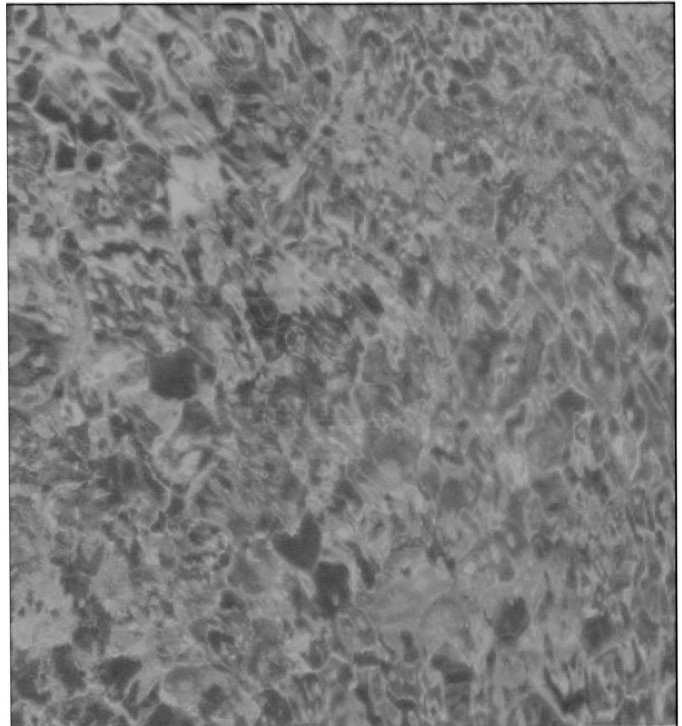

Made in the USA
Las Vegas, NV
23 September 2023